CH

Over in the Meadow

A COUNTING RHYME BY

Olive A. Wadsworth

ILLUSTRATED BY

Anna Vojtech

A CHESHIRE STUDIO BOOK

NorthSouth
BOOKS
New York · London

Over in the meadow…

. . . in the sand in the sun
Lived an old mother turtle
and her little turtle one.
Dig said the mother.
We dig said the one.
So they dug all day
in the sand in the sun.

Over in the meadow
where the stream runs blue
Lived an old mother fish
and her little fishes two.
Swim said the mother.
We swim said the two.
So they swam all day
where the stream runs blue.

Over in the meadow
in a hole in a tree
Lived an old mother owl
and her little owls three.
Tu-whoo said the mother.
Tu-whoo said the three.
So they tu-whooed
all day in a hole in a tree.

Over in the meadow
by the old barn door
Lived an old mother rat
and her little ratties four.
Gnaw said the mother.
We gnaw said the four.
So they gnawed all day
by the old barn door.

Over in the meadow
in a snug beehive
Lived an old mother bee
and her little bees five.
Buzz said the mother.
We buzz said the five.
So they buzzed all day
in a snug beehive.

Over in the meadow
in a nest built of sticks
Lived an old mother crow
and her little crows six.
Caw said the mother.
We caw said the six.
So they cawed all day
in a nest built of sticks.

Over in the meadow
where the grass grows so even
Lived an old mother frog
and her little froggies seven.
Jump said the mother.
We jump said the seven.
So they jumped all day
where the grass grows so even.

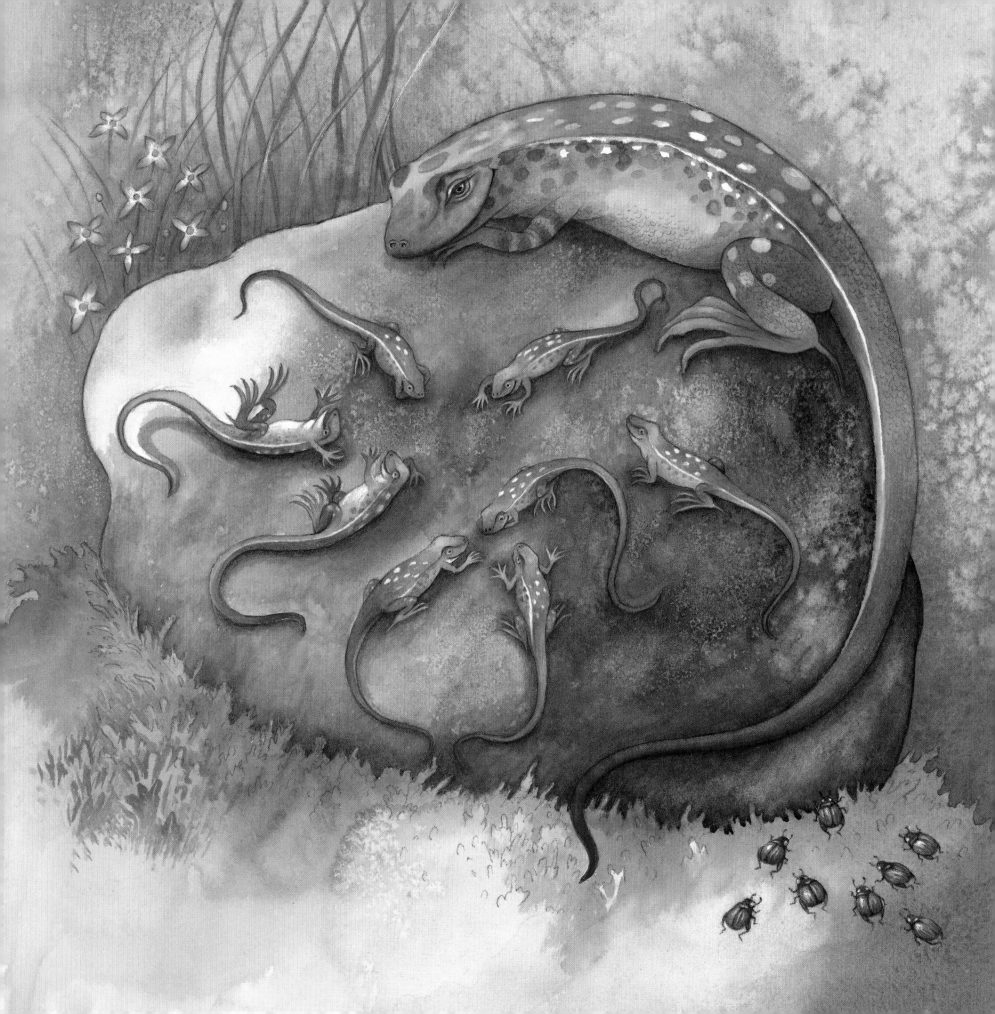

Over in the meadow
by the old mossy gate
Lived an old mother lizard
and her little lizards eight.
Bask said the mother.
We bask said the eight.
So they basked all day
by the old mossy gate.

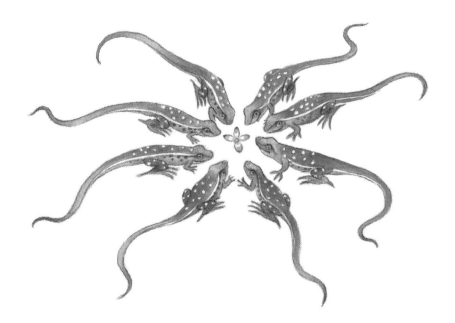

Over in the meadow
by the old Scotch pine
Lived an old mother duck
and her little ducks nine.
Quack said the mother.
We quack said the nine.
So they quacked all day
by the old Scotch pine.

Over in the meadow
in a cozy wee den
Lived an old mother beaver
and her little beavers ten.
Beave said the mother.
We beave said the ten.
So they beaved all day
in a cozy wee den.

FOR EMMA —A.V.

Published in the United States by North-South Books Inc., New York.
Published simultaneously in Great Britain, Canada, Australia, and New Zealand in 2002
by North-South Books, an imprint of NordSüd Verlag AG, Zürich, Switzerland.
First paperback edition published in 2003 by North-South Books.

Library of Congress Cataloging-in-Publication Data
Dana, Katharine Floyd, 1835–1886.
Over in the meadow: a counting rhyme / by Olive A. Wadsworth; illustrated by Anna Vojtech.
p. cm.
"A Cheshire Studio book."
Summary: A variety of meadow animals pursuing their daily activities introduce the numbers one through ten.
1. Nursery rhymes, American. 2. Children's poetry, American. 3. Animals—Juvenile poetry.
[1. Nursery rhymes. 2. American poetry. 3. Animals—Poetry. 4. Counting.]
I.Vojtech, Anna, ill. II. Title.
PS1499.D96 O97 2002 [E]—dc21 2001051434

A CIP catalogue record for this book is available from The British Library.

ISBN: 978-0-7358-1596-4 (TRADE EDITION)
5 7 9 HC 10 8 6 4
ISBN: 978-7358-1597-1 (LIBRARY EDITION)
1 3 5 7 9 LE 10 8 6 4 2
ISBN: 978-0-7358-1871-2 (PAPERBACK EDITION)
3 5 7 9 PB 10 8 6 4
Printed in Belgium